An Art, A Craft,
A Mystery

a novel in verse

Laura Secord

Livingston Press
The University of West Alabama

ISBN 13: trade paper 978-1-60489-303-8
ISBN 13: hardcover 978-1-60489-304-5
ISBN 13: e-book 978-1-60489-305-2

Library of Congress Control Number 2021953553
Printed on acid-free paper
Printed in the United States of America by
Publishers Graphics

Hardcover binding by: HF Group
Typesetting and page layout: Joe Taylor
Proofreading: Cassidy Pedram, Joe Taylor, McKenna Darley
Brooke Barger

Cover Art: Laura Secord

Cover design: Joe Taylor

Acknowledgments: on pages 178-182

Livingston Press is part of The University of West Alabama,
and thereby has non-profit status.
Donations are tax-deductible.
6 5 4 3 2 1

An Art, A Craft,
A Mystery

An Art, a Craft, a Mystery

We kept the small alive from day to day,
kept households warm, kept bread made.

While men sat in the meetinghouse
in ceaseless debate
on sin, redemption, destiny,
their grace came through women's works—
watching fires and keeping coals ablaze.
Their salvation came through women's hands,
gathering each day's yeasted scraps
for tomorrow's meal, a sacred pact.

Don't think these skills were simple,
they were an art, a craft, a mystery,
yet when the men took notice,
they doubted diligence and named it witchery.

Soul Mountain, Connecticut

Behind the trees, I heard
      the barking cries.
Two geese appeared,
      long-necked shadows crossing the slough—
Aunt Lydea, my cousin Kate—
      to me their stories flew.

Southwark of London, 1636

A Harpy

Lydea Gilbert

In our tenement we take in work—spinning.
With my husband again off to sea, I'm alone
with three wee-ones and niece, Kate,
married to someone I never see.

No kitchen. We buy our meals from the stalls in the streets.
Some evenings, I see that lone woman with burnt-red scars,
and those eyes, always drifting, part-crossed. Called a harpy,
she's hawking fruitcake squeezed in the shape

of a rose, and then shoved on a stick. Hear her shout—
Hallo! Ha-pence, ha-penny! Her eyes, how they mourn,
as she looks into me. I am choking. I tremble
and flee, slopping our stew on my skirts and my sleeves.

Hasty Rose Ring
Lydea Gilbert

One rosy morn in spring I find my man
home from the seas.   We celebrate and sing.
Our babies climb his lap;   he kisses me.
With a shilling from spinning, I buy us party treats—
     a special feast for Daddy's seadog yarns.
As children screech and giggle, he falls to coughing.

I'm hopeful wrapped in his arms.   A stifled cough,
shaking, his body shivers. I hold a sick man
at midnight, flushed with fever. I've heard sad yarns,
this one comes true. *My mates were ailing.*
     And still you sing?
     So glad to see our babies, I want to be their treat.
     I brew him tea and rub his back beside me.

Dawn finds me worried.   He spews his breakfast on me.
I wake up Kate.   *Watch them, I go to cure his cough.*
     I seek a chemist's syrup I hope will treat
his weakening, made from ginger to heal the man
I've longed for through two springs.   I sing
a prayer for healing.   By dusk, I see our family yarn

frays toward swelling grief.   Infested yarns
unravel all our joys.   *Kate, get these babies from me.*
Come, your Da needs sleep.   They huddle up while
Kate sings
     a ballad of love and loss as Richard coughs.
He's hellish hot and ringed with red.   This man
is dying.   A curse I can't begin to treat.

Time compresses.   Is this the death of which they sing?
     I turn to see my wee'uns failing.   Can't treat

them fast enough to save them.   All three coughing.
My Kate tries hard, we nurse them together.   Our yarn
        runs to its hasty end, where red rings glare at me.
Kate runs for help.   The Surgeon says, *It's plague.*
Shaken.   Can't sing.   I've lost my
man,
my babies.   No treatment worked by Kate or me.
We've lived the darkest tale, yet we're not coughing.

After the Plague
Lydea

My husband, dead. My babies gone. All love:
a failing.
>   *Why not me?*

To glorify their tender souls, I strive
to nurse those suffering and work to tend the living.
>   *Why not me?*

My Hal, my Viola, my Rosemary,
I nourish stranger's children in your names.
Sustain lives or witness their passing,
>   *Why not me?*

Through scourge infested alleys, Kate
and I cradle child after child, still this bane
of buboes, chills and fear subdues their frames.
>   *Why not mine?*

 Keeping memories alive, I cross
the lanes of hell.   Penance.
>   *Why not me?*

Passage

I.

Kate Gilbert

Aunt and I walk through our broken
neighborhood carrying herbs. We try
healing disease with no cure. This work
makes me forget, then re-live my cousins' dying.

Does she wish to pursue our lost
family? Nurture in murderous
hovels — her solution to everything
crumbling. We'll nurse others, die or live.

II.

Lydea

So alone: Kate and I.
This tenement room
could not contain the pain
shooting like flames
down my neck and arms.
Even my face feels
smeared with sorrow.

I could not stand
my feet touching the streets,
after many funeral pyres.
Kate touched my face.
Her hands burned me.

I knew I needed sea,
and cold salt-spray against what we have seen.
I told Kate I was going to find us food,
but went down to the docks, and sold ourselves for

passage on ship Truelove.

...to the Colonies—worlds unknown, where family lives.
Gather our poor things, we take to sea come the morning.

Aboard The Truelove 1636

Self-sold and Adrift
Lydea

Last night on stormy seas, a young
girl jumped the ship.
Kate and I, lost limbs of a broken family,
float on this vast ocean. I mount the stair
to walk the deck and look across the water,

recall my Grandmam as she combed my tangled
hair. *Be still. Listen. Your people are ancient*
folk, who find divinity in all things. At ten,
I gazed across the ocean, wondering how
the cloaked night, a cobalt blanket sewn
with light, could be so vast, and cover all the sea.

A gull calls. He rounds the mast, hunting
for a bite of fish or meat—yet turns away
from the moldy oatcake I toss him.

Self-sold and adrift to unknown lands.
My faith is finding cousins where we travel,
but the distance between is just gray
water reflecting the sky's darkening.

A Little Entertainment
Kate

Below in this dark ship, crowded
like pease in a barrel, are many
tired women, restless men, wet-nosed,
crying children, and some who answer every need
with prayer after prayer.

Nights I climb up to the deck,
and ponder the bright skies.

I avoid men's eyes, but the ship's
boy comes to me. *D'ya read Miss?*
Aunt Lydea taught me secretly.

I nod in reply. From his bag he pulls
a book—William Lilley's *Christian Astrology.*
*I ca'not, but one said this book tells stories
of the stars, and you seem so fond of them.*

Labor and Delivery

I.

Lydea

With little room for even a bit of privacy,
I bribe the mate with ginger sticks to help
me prepare a travail place for a frightened
girl to have her baby.

We hang scrap sails, fill the space
with straw and shavings, make plans to heat
the water. *Brackish will do if boiled.*

We stitch sheets with torn bedclothes,
and with any willing woman's skirt scraps.

The red-haired Irish sailor says I make him recall
the Papist Sisters, for I am so determined in my work.
I begin to teach the birth breath,
and assure her green husband all
can be safe, even with the tossing waves.

II.

Kate

I worried all these past days that Molly,
        huge-bellied, hardly able to walk,
and making water constantly, would birth
        her child on these rough seas.

Her pains began on wild waters,
        all in darkness this past night.
Aunt and I had just prepared a place
        in the storage of the ship's bow.

Molly's eyes were full of dread, but Lydea,

with a clear, direct voice, instructed well,
helping her to birth without a tear.

All the passengers are now amazed. They expected
          screams of pain, but only heard
the deep breath, the fast breath, the dog's pant-
          as we told her, *Push. Push now*,
then a healthy son's lusty cries.
          He sucks teat mighty well.

In The House of
Mistress Anne Hutchinson

Ashore

Lydea

Lined up. Groups of local Masters needing
servants judge us, looking to choose some sea-worn
drudge for temporary bondage—this servitude will
pay our passage.

Here in Massachusetts Bay,
indentured labor builds two-storied
homes and cares for children, farms the Masters'
lands, and helps to create a thriving colony.

The Captain means to trade us, pointing at me—
*Widow, strong-boned, works hard, plus this
junior maiden.*

I am praying no one
splits us. I concentrate and focus deep,
direct into these merchant's eyes, with silent pleas
to keep us together.

Looking with kindness,
the Merchant Hutchinson now speaks, *I'll
take these two, the matron, her girl.*

This Untamed Place
Lydea

I love this wild place. The air smells
ever green, and trees outnumber men.
At night, I hear zephyrs whispering the leaves,
and think we have landed in a paradise,
where grace is crimson across ridges
and blows across this untamed space.

Sabbaths, we sit for hours in the meetinghouse.
In back, the women's side, classed by sex
and name. I drift from the preacher's doom,
doubting his message. So much concern for thoughts
of evil, blind to the good in everything.

Through Daily Labors
Lydea

I follow Mistress Anne, a dance through daily
tasks, she paints with thoughts, talks and challenges.
Noticing my skills attending women's labor,
sickness, pain and healing, she asked me to
work along beside her.

Always she prays ahead of entering
a household door. Before we go inside,
she'll fan her Bible till she feels the Holy Ghost
reveal a verse which speaks to our trail ahead.

Today, she read, *I fear no evil, Thou art with me; Thy rod, Thy
staff comfort me.* Standing before the threshold,
Mistress spoke, *This birth will be hard but the mother
will be well, a healthy child delivered.*

Making clean, we started our tasks—her ear to
baby's heart. Observing pain and breath, she softly
spoke, to ease the mother's fears—*Don't worry;
God's with you. His hands will guide your baby.*

The mother's breath then slowed quite steady, bearing
labor's push with grace, as Mistress Anne predicted.

The Hutchinson Debate

Henry Vane   vs   *John Winthrop*

Come Along, I'll bring you to a woman who preaches better gospel than your black-coats—	Her dangerous errors
a woman of another kind of spirit, who has had many revelations;	Overstepped the boundaries from the kitchen and nursery,
Renown as a sympathetic healer, capable of helping women raise families in this hostile world..	An open door to sin
A woman who healed them, who talked to them, who led them. Endowed with magnetism—	She supersedes the Bible, Church and Ministers Breeder and nourisher of distemper
As much as eighty women come to her hanging on her every word.	More bold than any man, resolving doctrine, explaining scripture:
One with God's grace in their heart cannot go astray.	
Laws and edicts are for those with a personal union with the Holy Ghost,	Ideas proper only for men, stronger minds. This assertion of personal communion with God is rebellion,
the free gift of God's grace,	needs strict discipline

membership in the covenant of grace.

                                      is not for the disorderly,

Her knowledge comes from revelation,

                                      with cunningly colored

                                      opinons.

serene enough in her faith. She will

will never doubt the state of her soul.

                                      It's time for this woman
                                      to be subdued once and
                                           for all.

The Trial of Anne Hutchinson
1637

Before Ministers and Magistrates
Kate

Mistress Anne is going on trial
for heresy at the Cambridge meetinghouse.
Her toddler, Zuriel, still nurses at night,
so I was chosen to come along, and watch
him at her eldest daughter's home.

His mam already kissed his head good-bye,
but he's restless, and our calming walk
leads us to the meetinghouse door.

The hall is filled. I stand beside the cracked
daub 'round the window frame and peer
inside. The Magistrates and Ministers are dressed
in solemnity, yet the throng outside is noisy as a carnival.

I hear the Crier announce,
Goodwife Anne Hutchinson,
and then I see her,
pale, yet all her own self—
walking, head high, eyes
direct, into that empty place
where she will stand before them.

Zuriel clings in my arms,
his heart races,
but he stays quiet.

Then all those that love her—
The women she has nursed and midwifed,
women and men enraptured by her sermons
at her weekly conventicles—
begin to shout and cheer.

I want to know her fearlessness.

Zuriel trembles, as if to whimper,

I stroke his arm,
                mutter kisses to his face.

She stands alone, while those that judge
are seated with warm coals around their feet.

What have I said or done?
She asks this
of our Governor once,
and once again,
What law do I transgress?

        I feel Zuriel squirming, and I do not want
              Mistress to notice,
        so I take the baby before the sea,
           and we twirl,
          while his Mother's ordeal
           spins before us—
waves, homes, hills, forest, skies, and her billowing courage,
        as Zuriel squeals with delight.

A False Wall
Kate

They assisted Mistress home,
cheeks blanched. She stumbled
before her daughter caught her fall.

Master told us how she'd fainted, but determined
she stood herself up again. Her weakening
caused the Magistrates to call an end
to the proceedings for the day.

I bring her herbs, steeped in a tea.
She smiles wanly and swallows the warm brew.
> *I've not confided my condition, but you've*
> *noticed I'm with child, so lavender*
> *and skullcap — good choice.*

I lift her hair, and swab
the line of her neck.
> *I fight against a false wall built*
> *by those who wish dominion over thought,*
> *yet God's truth lives beyond the meetinghouse.*

I stroke her forehead with a cool cloth.

> *And yet, I am trapped. I must use the swords of Scripture,*
> *knowledge and reason against a wall as unmoving as brick.*

I fix her coif over her cleansed neck,
> *You are wise and kind. Now bring Zuriel*
> *to me, so he can nurse and I can sleep.*

Her plump and joyous toddler
in her arms all walls melt
here in soft and yielding love.

To Break Her
Lydea

Mistress Anne is in bondage,
under house arrest at the home of a Minister.

Bereft, Master comes to get her things.
Not her husband or her children are allowed
to see her for four months. She will sit alone
in a plain room, with no work to free her mind.

They plan to break her, reduce her,
force her to let go of her ideals
and lay herself open to the clergy.

My mind sees her in repose, lit by a light shaft
from an attic window—fearless daughter
and ardent servant to His word, believer
that all have a right to His love, even woman,
even servant girl.

I see her floating in a boat of grace—
confident, innocent, naked, afloat on her truths.
Doubtless, even in her suffering and isolation,
willing to endure any punishment to confirm her faith.

Anne Hutchinson
Banished 1638

Released

Lydea

After months not seeing her children,
Mistress Anne's released.

Little ones gather around her. Into her arms
she pulls them. Her voice stirs up a bowl of tears.

> *The men have decided, my loves. We must pack*
> *and leave at dawn to cross the snowy frontier.*

The little ones begin to whimper.
I can see her pallid weakness.

> *Lydea, we cannot take you or Kate.*
> *I can give you freedom, there is little else.*

She takes my hands, whispers thanks,
eats in silence and studies the flames.

Walk

Kate

We watch
        Mistress
          and children

begin their walk
          across
               snowy land.

Something   in me
          wants to beg,
            follow.

She is known,
          well familiar,

yet I
          do not complain
              or plead.

Wounded Ally

Lydea

We have freedom. Still, we are chickens in a pen,
with five schillings and the clothes on our backs,
waiting for the fox to find our weakness.

Troubles clinging, I encounter my husband's
nephew, Thomas, just disembarked—
hungry, cold, forlorn, clothes in tatters.

Over a meal and a draught. I listen
to his tale, told over the rough
alehouse boards. He'd stayed behind in Yardley

till his beloved's father gave consent
for marriage. Her eyes were like violets, so he waited.
Their daughter was newborn when they boarded

the doomed vessel. Both died before landfall.
Now, he plans to cross this snow—a hundred
miles to Hartford, where our family waits.

I take him to Kate, younger cousin, still fanciful
in brightening beauty. With destinies
unknown, the three of us elect to travel together.

A Far Leap

Kate

Almost as suddenly as we lose our place
with Mistress Hutchinson, I find Lydea
has arrived with cousin Thomas. *Ah,*
Katy-kin, you've grown.

I say good-bye to the gables, the fine
glass windows, strong bricks
and the view of the sea.

Lydea wraps our feet in extra rags
to protect against the miles of snow.
I leap onto the unknown path before me.

To The Great River Valley

I.

Lydea

We trek the frozen winter lands.
Our scout, a Native man employed
by Thomas, leads us, walks undaunted,
keeps a pace, remains in sight. At night,

he shows us forest ways—builds
us shelter, uncovers alcoves
concealed amid the brush and snow.

He never seems to feel the sting
of cold. Without a gripe, without
complaint, he becomes our signal fire.

He walks with inner stillness, while
we toil—the contest, true—to learn
endurance through the harshest things.

II.

Kate

I was nine, living with my cousins,
near the river Severn's snaky blue meander.
After a thick and deep snow, quick as the blow
had ceased, we tramped above the whitened
valley. We counted arches, spires, villages,
iced water-wheels and the pale mountains.
Walking west, I again pretend
my arms are wings, remembering telling cousins,
Let's be crows, and imagine flying
overland to view frosted hills and farms—

soaring, to find a roofless hut,
peering at table, stool, bed, candles
and plates, coated in glistened light. My air-
borne feet leave hollows in the mounded white.

Reunion

Lydea

At the family settlement
beside the Great River,
we're given dry clothes,
fed warm pottage,
squeezed around the kitchen—
with in-laws, nephews, Jonathan,
Josiah and Sarah, my niece.

I sense Thomas set apart, until his mother hears
his story: his wife's death and the loss
of her first grandchild.

I lie awake in a crowd of pallets
on the floor, wonder how we'll fit
into this temporary home.
Will we only feel like extra mouths?

Two Positions
Lydea

Jonathan has found us two positions,
one north, in Windsor, and one at a Captain's
house in Hartford Town. I want us
together. I long to speak
against it, but decline.

Kate— young and bold
is excited about the large house,
and making friends with other girls.

I lose my precious strong-willed girl
hoping that she'll be wise enough
to hearken to life's dangers.

Windsor 1640

The Widower
Lydea

When he lost his wife and son, Henry Stiles built grief.
Sickness killed them with bloody coughs, spilling grief.

Though his church does not allow it, saying
God's plans can't be questioned, he dwells in grief.

Though sorrow's idle and tainted with evil, he can't be done.
Though it's not, and will never be, *His Will* to grieve.

Eating poorly, leaving his fields untended, and his cows,
their udders almost bursting, not milked and ever filling: his
grief.

Below the rocky hill, above the marshy meadows, his family
summon help from those Gilberts not kilt by grieving.

Ever seeking a new future, Thomas asks if I will join him.
Lydea gladly answers, her heart's instilled with grief.

Below the Ground
Lydea

Thomas and I serve Henry Stiles,
a marsh away from the Great River
in a cellar house, dug half-
way in the ground—slat shingles,
one door, two low windows,
two placed high to draw
smoke like a chimney, an open fire
pit—daub walls blackened.
I, tending three fires at once,
can spit-roast, stew and bake.

Outdoors—untended gardens, weedy
corne and pease, thorny meadows for the stock.
We strive and toil for Stiles' farm, hoping
Thomas will earn a patch of land,
yet to move about a place, where my hands
can touch and bend, and my influence
amend such neglected beauty, gratifies my days.

A Few Things
Lydea

Upon the shelf in Stiles' seler house,
above the table and beside the fire,
I keep my few things—a green glass
bottle of colony vinegar—small beer
capped by scraps of linen cloth and left
to sour in the sun—an earthen candle stick,
a metal plate, a wooden trencher. Hanging
below—strings of onion, feverfew,
calendula and sage. As windows offer little light,
we keep the door thrown open when
the shadows blanket night, and the fire's banked.
I spread my pallet down below the men's
bed, where the waxing moon casts monthly
floodlight shadows, and lengthens my repas

House of Captain Cullick
Hartford 1640

My New Life
Kate

After being in close quarters for so long,
I leap at the offer to live on my own.
I'm near grown, yet Lydea directs—
        Learn to hold thy tongue.

My mother died in my birth,
my father died at sea, orphaned
as I was born, Aunt Lydea chose
my name for me. She was solid, strict and kind,

yet she chose my Christian name from a playhouse
comedie: *A heroine with her own voice,
a bold lass who spoke freely.*
        Still she bossed me.

This big house in Hartford, is happiness,
with three other girls, sleeping in the garret, amid
barrels of Indian corne and pease, two spinning
wheels and blue flax fields as far as eyes can see.

The Captain leads us all in supper prayer,
Mistress and their daughter seated at the table,
servants standing by the wall. But at night

we low girls make our own way,
in stories spun, in fancies milked,
in dreams unfurled like cloth.

Storied Talk
Kate

Mistress Cullick talks and talks,
chattering all through the prescribed time
for our edification. Her *ladies-in-waiting*, she calls
us, though we're not ladies, only servant girls,
who she trains in embroidery skills
each afternoon, once our toil's temporarily complete.

Our days begin in darkness, where we complete
first chores—start the fire, gather eggs—no talking
till the Captain and Mistress awake. They critique our skill
at serving them like Lords and Ladies spending time
on a wilderness holiday. Mistress gathers her girls,
after the midday meal is served and cleared, calling

Come, come, the light is right for sewing. Mistress calls
my handwork atrocious. It's never complete,
for she makes me pull my threads out. *My worst girl.*
I turn her strident voice, incessant talk off—
how her noble Captain wasted no time
in burning out the Pequot tribe. His skills

in killing savages highly praised—*Commend his skill,
and social standing, when talking
to a man.* I don't finish my sampler in time,
my threads leave holes in the linen. I'll never compete.
The sunlight fades. I hear the cows call
for milking, the pigs for slop. Just a low girl

once again. After dark, I become another girl
who pretends among her peers to have a skill
with fortune-telling. Our pallets spread, we talk.
I tell the story of a crone who called
me over, and sold me a package complete
with gilded letters writ: *Money Rain*. Stuffed with thyme,

I thought it predicted prosperous times,
but I've remained a lowly serving girl.

I offer fortunes from my book of astrology, and complete
each with some lucky fate. Let them believe my skill.
Let them think that I am more than what Mistress calls
me.   Creating new worlds in our attic talks,

fantastic visions completed with my special skill—
painting pictures of girls with futures called
well-wrought—I elevate myself with storied talk.

A Visit

Kate

Jonathan takes me to visit Lydea
in Windsor. By the fire-pit in a seler house,
there's one chair, the Goodman's seat,
where Lydea sits me. She tends her fires—
the iron turnip pot, the trussed fowl
she turns over a bed of coals, the clay
box where bread bakes— while I remember

her stories. In childhood, she'd sit me down,
a bowl of pease to shell, while she would weave—
tales of the little man who gave a poor
girl power to spin straw to gold;
of a rose red girl, whose sweetness made her words
fall from her mouth as rubies; of the man turned
to a donkey by fairies, and of the girl lost at sea, who dressed
herself as a boy, yet found true love—

Our blue bowl full of pease, my mind running
down old paths of fantasy. Now she's
telling me, "I love this place. In the garden
I see Viola, Hal and Rosemary
catching dazzling bugs to show me".

I don't want to think of lost things any longer.
This is a poor place—crunchy ashes in the baking.
Yet, I cannot call the Cullicks' place
my home—inside its walls there's nothing that I own.

Life in Windsor 1640-1650

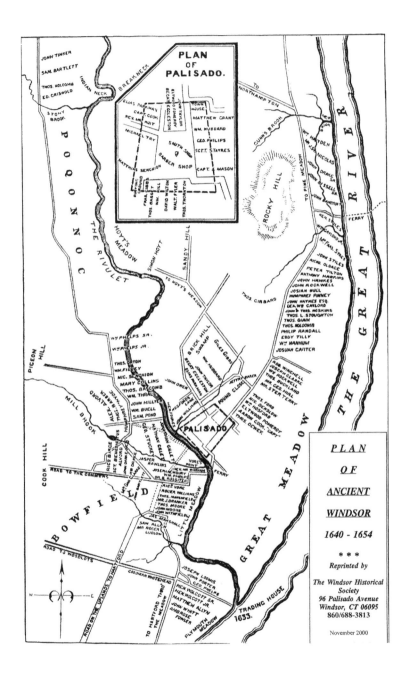

PLAN OF PALISADO.

PLAN
OF
ANCIENT
WINDSOR
1640 - 1654

* * *

Reprinted by

The Windsor Historical
Society
96 Palisado Avenue
Windsor, CT 06095
860/688-3813

November 2000

Midwife

Lydea

Up and down this river are folks who settled
years before my coming. Some seemed
cold towards me, only a servant, but with healing
skills, I began to warm them.

In status, I was naked, had no husband,
land or title, but I carried gifts nursing
through labor and sickness. This opened doors
and let me near their bedsides.

Plain and simple as I seemed,
I sat long hours in attendance,
lighting dark, untangling agonies,
and guiding steady through labyrinths
made of births, deaths, the pain of injury,
the cramp of flux, fear's misery.

Tender Thoughts

Lydea's giant turnip

My growing greens
she harvests leaf by leaf.
She circles fingers round my belly,
swollen fat above black earth, and adores
my pearly rose skin. She will not pull me,
though voices criticize.

She harvests my leaves, wilts them
with game fat and sweet onion,
but releases my core to soil's blanket.

I promise her I'll birth new greens in spring.
She packs me in soft loam and moss,
protects me from the killing frosts.
My plan—to share my tenderness
through seasons of maternity.

.

A Birth Confession
Lydea

I attend an unmarried girl's labor, the servant
to Goodman Hoyte. From a bitter wind
and blowing snows, Hoyte drags me in the door,
directing me to make her pain's sting
force her to confess the father's name.

I will not pay some bastard's keep.

I'm a midwife, not confessor, but I'll try.

She lies amid seed bags — the granary, her childbed.
She's so young, and her eyes beg me for help.
I, alone, assist — massaging her belly, back
and shoulders with a salve from red-gold flowers.

I sing, in the tempo of a hymn, not a psalm, but a folk
song from old Cornwall, a children's song
about dancing in the sun. My vision comes
through touching her. I see her shame—
Hoyte's eldest son, the root cellar, her failed struggle.

The other women come to assist and witness
her worse pains. I pretend to question her
mightily as her birthing pangs mount.

She screams, but never answers, cries
and trembles, still breathless in her uncertain fate.

She delivers a boy with a tuft of carrot hair,
an exact match to Hoyte's son. No confession required.

I wipe him dry, swaddle and fix him to her breast,
while the murmurs 'round the fireside divulge the truth.

Sequester Meadow
Lydea

After snowmelt in the spring we found a swamp
with mud so deep the ox sank to its knees.
The three of us released him, dragging hempen line.

My shoes and skirts clotted down with mud.

As I led the ox away from the sucking earth,
I saw a tiny face float up into the muddy
pool—the clean skull of an infant.

Why here, in this fickle, flooding meadow?

Imagining a babe carried away
from its mother in an angry flood, I reached
to save it, but it was drawn back by the soggy muck—

its small white visage disappearing into rusty ground.

Bissell's Ferry
Lydea

I.
Goodman Bissell's built a ferry, and yesterday
we moved the stock to eastern pastures.
Great oxen were roped to either end;
Bissell and his sons directed the pulling.
Standing dead center, I kept the stock calm.

Goodwife Bissell and I packed food
enough for all, cold pottage, cheese,
biscuits and small beer—a celebration.
The men were delighted. I was pleasured by the trip
across the river—the deep water, the forested
and rocky sides, the hawk's cry overhead.

II.
I brave the ferry many times, when Thomas
and the men stay on the eastern side. I hear
the bell toll, put on a heavy cloak and walk to shore.

Masked in meekness, I meet the travelers—
sometimes trappers back from Massachusetts Bay,
sometimes the citizens of our little town,
and even Natives, cooler in their disposition
than I, but just as masked.

I load the ferry, and ring the bell again.
I hold us still along the rope line
across the winter's waters. Sometimes
I'm followed by the moon, sometimes
the storms make the river turbulent,
sometimes these passengers speak,
and I am entertained with stories.

Though it's a kindness, a labor that needs doing,

a service to all travelers; some complain
about a woman guiding folk across a river
as if it were a devil's deed.

A Lashing

Lydea

I am called to the house of Goodman H.D.
to dress the whip marks on his wife's back.

The court ordered six stripes to her naked back
in a public display on the Palisado Green
as punishment for a voice too brash and harsh.

Standing at a distance, I saw the crowd
gather 'round her small frame, men
with muskets ready, and women glaring.

As they flogged her bare skin, her arms
fought bravely to cover her breasts.

Now the wounds have festered, angry red, and leaking
amber pus. I warm water and loosen
her shift's ripped threads stuck deep in the whip's
ruptures.
    She bursts apart with tears.

    Let them flow.
    Cleanse that memory.

I pack her wounds with linen smeared
in calendula and goose fat.

    It took courage
    to endure such shame.

Oh, the same true voice that gives a man great glory
brings the pain and sorrow we women suffer for.

To the Hutchinson Children

New Amsterdam

Deare Ones

Word at the meetinghouse is your mother was killed by natives. Reverend maintains God took wrath against her, but her God was not wrathful. She carried Him in her kind love for the natives, who taught her to use mullein, blueberries, sage and sugar maple trees. I feel she died in gratitude to give her life for the English trespasses against these peoples. Never forget her gentle hands on your forehead and her kind whispers when she held a mother's grief. She could turn a psalm to a lullaby and back again…

Lydea Gilbert 1644
Windsor Connecticut

Accusation 1648
Lydea

I saw them take Alyse Young and drag
her away in chains, to be tried for witchcraft.

Last March, we trudged the snows to nurse
the town through shaking chills, coughs and fevers.

When illness caught her, I came to her, soothed
her chest with cedar poultice, made her tea

from wild ginger, kept her fire, fed her family,
did her spinning. As she healed, the light

returned to her eyes and glossed her auburn
hair. She shared her seclusion

as a young wife in this village, wanting to teach
her daughter old-world fairy stories

and celebrate her singing, when no one
here approves delight's imaginings.

Hartford 1650

Gathering Ballad
Kate

A burst of spring came to the glade,
with tiny blossoms forming,
I grabbed a basket and a blade,
got leave to go out gathering.

Discovered chestnuts in their shells,
and found fresh sprouts of garlic,
I picked new mushrooms by the well,
and wandered deeper, gathering.

I walked beside the tumbling stream,
that rushes for the river, and sat
upon a granite stone to see
the man I treasured—

craftsman, shipwright
Jonathan—building boats
along his slipway
across the golden water.

I knew his walk, hair dark, gait tall,
and watched him guide his workers.
They sawed a stack of chestnut trunks,
then pegged them down a sloop's hull.

I reached inside my pocket
to give some time to stitching.
I worked my needle, making
red sprigs on poesied linen

O Cousin, lift your eyes and see
me smiling in these trees. Just look
my way, just cast your gaze.
I beg you wave me over.

My needle slipped and pierced my palm,
unleashing drips of crimson. *Oh, Jonathan,*

I'll be your love, this secret song
came warbling from my tongue.

I saw him wave his hand,
I thought I saw him call. Stuffed
my pocket, left my yarns,
and dashed to him;

Out the forest, I crossed the bridge, and darted
like an arrow, paying no heed as mud
splashed my skirts, I leapt
for him with a fractured basket.

Cousin, why so far from home?
What brings you here, your jacket torn?
I stood alone, a tousled girl,
his men all came around.

Ashamed and wrong my face grew hot.
I must escort my cousin home.
He marched me down the road around the forest.
Young kin, you must conduct yourself to fit your station.

My pace grew slow. I sucked my sleeve
where blood spots still adorned it.
A foolish child, to hear his plea—
I'm only worried for you.

Back home, with naught to show—
except a barren basket,
my cousin tipped his hat and walked,
not looking back, without a thought, for me.

to Lydea Gilbert

Deare Aunt

Jonathan came to the Cullicks. Mistress allowed me to go riding with him and his friend, John Harrison— tall, rust hair, blue eyes. We toured the land in Wether's Field, where Harrison resides. Jonathan's purchased an Ordinary. Harrison will grow the hops, barley and tobacco. Harrison smiled, looking at me when we parted.

Kate Gilbert
10 May 1650

Uncaged

Kate

I'm a bird loosed from a cage—
John's found me.
he owns his piece of land, a house
with two rooms, a garret,
an oven and an orchard.
Wethersfield's crier,
his voice is laughing deep.

He doesn't mind
that I can read, and write well, too.
I speak to him with ease.

When his hand
touches mine, I feel a thrill;
when I hear him call my name,
I grow both tall and still.

A Proposal

Kate

John comes alone.
I'm serving.
After waiting, he passes a parchment
scrap to the Captain.

On John's mount,
        we ride.
At an outcropping above the river,
        he swings me to the ground,
        and walks me between two large oaks.

I'm astounded, as he kneels,

I can no longer wait, please, be my love, marry me.

I long to bring myself
        close to him.
I drop down to my knees
        so we are face to face again.

        My heart sings when I'm with you.

Then partners, helpmates, in affection we shall be.

Haloed by Firelight
Kate

I have waited. I am quite grown,
and have heard the growls
and hammerings of night beds
all my days. Time now for me.

He brings me before the fire,
covering my face in gentle
touches from his lips,
like bird wings and butterflies.

Slowly and with kisses, he unties
and unlashes my white
wool vest, and my stiff
cream petticoats,
till I only wear my linen shift.

My love slides hands beneath, and
up my thigh, my hip, my belly, and my breasts,
so lightly, he leaves me all in tingles,
so deep in longing, that I murmur,
moan, then cry and cry again.
A band of unfamiliar music,
an orchestration,
in jubilation calls.

Devoted

Kate

Such affection fills us. Every
task becomes my greater joy.

In town they call him Crier. Gifted.
Thundervoice. For me his words

are soft as summer rain, beguiling,
our own choice. While newly-wed,

he asks to spill his seed against
my thigh, to give us time to live our

days as paramours
before a baby turns our eyes away

from loving. Plotting time to stay
devoted, only to each other.

Henry Stiles 1651

Early Windsor: *Henry Stiles*

I.
1634: Settlement

10 May   Francis agreed to act as emissary for Lord
              Saltonstall.
              Come dawn we sail to the Colonies to claim the
              land grant.

16 Oct   We disembark after seas and a great river, my
              brother Francis tells the settlers to call him
              Lord.

18 Oct   Given dead-Indian land — a village passed
              away, victims of a trader's plague — the
              jaundice dropsy.

20 Oct   Our Providence. The native stores — grain, beans,
              squash, dried fish, jerky, hides and pottery —
              their fire-pits and tilled fields.

31 Oct   Last night a screaming wind. Tortured souls
              and children's ghostly cries. Unsettling.

II.
1636: Trade

2 Sep   Floods and failed crops. Our native stores are spent.

5 Nov   Cursed. We are starving.

12 Nov   Traded my musket to an Indian for
              ground corne and a share of hunted game.

15 Nov   My brother feasts on my venison and fritters
              with red-tree syrup, I tell him of the barter.

24 Nov   Francis complains to the court about my bargain—

25 Nov   A day shackled in the stocks.

18 Feb   The Indian keeps leaving waterfowl on my door. Francis feeds his family the meat of my disgrace.

Demanding Tribute
Lydea

Francis always has his eyes on Henry,
making constant inquiries.

He drops by for refreshment.
Henry is generous,

asking me to bring his brother
a flagon of the best ale.

I serve, and listen consciously.

—*Your pasture?*
    —*Thick with new wheat.*
—*The land along the river?*
    —*So thick with corne, you cannot see. Thomas*
    and I, together, have done the work of three.
—*And your larders?*
    —*Good Lydea has filled them with linen cloth*
    and cheese.

How can a younger brother demand such accounting?

Thomas holds his tongue, determined to buy
a piece of land from Francis outright,

Francis acts like the Babylonian king, and we,
his enchained drudges, trading tributes for survival.

—*I want to taste your cheeses*, he orders me.
Henry nods—I carry back a round from the buttery.

Francis wraps it, fills his side pouch, stands to leave.
—*Work a little harder brother, and we'll see.*

When he's gone, I rinse his flagon and set it in the sun.
Let light burn off the remnants of his touch.

Spider Sonnet

Lydea

I dream I wake to see our grain barrels wrapped
in spiders, long legs draped over the lids.
Serve cheese instead, I think, but the rounds
are shimmering, covered in eight-legged creatures.

I sit to study them—Fat bodies with soft
hairs, legs striped in shades of black
and brown, over every cup, barrel, tub and flask.

Some might think to destroy them, but these
same spinners, create webs—dressed in dew
like diamonds—catch flies in their threshold
nets, are relaxed and resplendent across the larders.

I choose to stay and offer admiration, and as I do,
they lift on strands of silken thread, off the corne
and barley, wheels of cheese, as if protecting me.

Cleaning Garlic

Henry

*A late summer's evening. I sat on the bench end, greasing
my boots. Lydea joined me, her basket filled with dried garlic.
The western sun sent streaks across our labors. I watched
her hands—rubbing the bulbs free of papery skins, clipping
the root hairs with her knife. Swallows dove in the falling
light. She found a steady pace—hand to bulb, filling a bowl
with brittle moon-paper petals, and a basket with trimmed
heads for fall storage. Above her ever-moving fingers, one
chestnut strand, streaked with silver light, swung from her
cap. I almost caught her eye—but my sight stayed enraptured
with her steady hands, filling containers with light.*

Sonnet for Henry
Lydea

As dawn seeps through the winter sky,
I watch a squirrel traverse dark branches.

I work too hard to note old heartaches' cries.
I journeyed far pursuing second chances,
yet find my waiting hours lasting years.

From fire-to-fire, meal-to-meal, I plod,
counting rosy sunrise against those morns
with bleary skies. No time for sobbing.

I never spoke the swellings in my breast
or reached outside my heart for honest touch—
just stocked the larders, choking up my chest.

For long I've known a woman can't ask much
but a dry cot and small beer come the dusk.
For years, abiding, till now I see I'm loved.

If This Be Heresy
Lydea

O Henry, once as cold as craggy peak—
Stony man, you never seemed to seek

life's honey, but look, you went to seek
fistfuls of autumn flowers from our meadow.

Come down from bloomy places on our meadow—
Find an empty flagon. I've poesies for your table.

I cannot match their beauty at this table.
The meal today is but yesterday's bread,

eggs from the ashes, turnip mashed bread.
They don't complain and eat hearty.

In fading light on this rich night, heartily
we make one family and celebration carries.

None cares if this be heresy; our laughter carries.
O Henry, nothing cold as craggy peak.

Death's Echo

3rd October 1651. Henry Stiles of Windsor is killed when the gun of Thomas Allyn, also of Windsor, accidentally discharges during a militia exercise.

Lydea

Four men carry his body, the stretcher rocking.
His rock-gray arm is lifeless.

His life leapt with that blood-red blast,
bursting from his heart. Ripped to shreds.

Shredded sanguine linen and wool.
Wooly hairs saturate his chest.

Chased from my life by a musket ball.
Bald truths never before spoken,

spoken face-to-face for this fortnight.
O nights of sworn affection and promises.

All promise broken. Doomed, we spoke with honest hearts.
His heart, swollen with love's professions,

will profess in loving tones no more.
Must I know more, and still prepare his body?

This body I held for just a palm-full of nights.
Nights of full moon and filled arms—

arms embracing me, unleashed.
Now, I am leashed to pain.

With painful memory and recollection,
I collect warm water and rags.

His body, like a stiff rag lies upon the table.
Time to table your dreams.

Never dreamed l would remove his bloody clothing,
now, his bloody clothing I withdraw with care,

caring nothing for my flooding tears.

Tears mingle in the wash water,

on watery rags, rung damp. Start here.
Here, his eyes closed. Black lashes. A crag of nose.

His nose against my cheek. All life gone.
Gone, the brass buttons I sewed on.

I cannot sew back his exploded breast.
In my breast, I feel his whisper.

Lydea, whispered. His last breath.
His breath speaking one last word, my name.

Naming love was his final act.
Act less broken, I tell myself.

Selvage fabric twined with skin.
Skin exposed, sliding his breeches away.

Is there no other way? No, I must witness all,
bless every part. How might I...

Might I come back to his hands?
They were handy with a hemp knot,

they were not mine, but known by me.
Mean and vengeful fate.

Fated we were to speak too late.
Late.   Eternally.

Evicted

Lydea

I.

Like tree limbs hung with pitchers
full of tears, tossed and sloshing in the wind,
more troubles begin.

Francis Stiles comes early as I am going
to milk. He asks for a drink. I search for a small
beer, sensing the cow udders aching.

Thomas stands. I serve. Francis gives orders.
He's sold our land and cellar, we must vacate
in a fortnight. His men will come for Henry's
estate—everything around us—built
with our own hands.

Thomas asks, *What of our work these past years?*
Francis states, *Never enough.*

With Francis gone, Thomas brings me parchment
and quill, along with my book of our accounts.
We shall claim our debt, what Henry Stiles' estate
owes us for our labor, and all we spent to make this farm.

I ask Thomas to relieve the cows
and settle into Henry's chair to write:

II.

An Account of Debts Due
       from Henry Stiles to Thomas Gilbert—

Three shillings per week for his diet,
eight yards of cloth and
making two shirts   *£19, 16 s*

Lent in wheat   *2 bush. and 3 pecks*
Lent in pease   *4 bush. and 1/2 peck*

96

Lent in oats		*4 bush*
Paid	*to Thos Hoskins for him*	*4 s*
	to John Eggleston for him	*4 s*
	to John Bancroft for him	*4 s*
	to John Drake junior for him and	*4 s*
Paid to John Densler for him		*£1*
For cloth for two shirts		*4 s*
For a cotton jacket		*8 s*

*For 28 days work about building
his cow house and cellar*   *£2 2 s*

*For eight days work of my self and cattle
to draw timber, stone and straw
around ye buildings*   *£1 1s*

*For thirty days work about fencing
stuffe over the river*   *£3 35s*

For thirty weeks of diet for John Burton   *£2 2s*

*For John Burton's wages and dieting
at harvest time for two harvest seasons*   *£1 6s*

Total   *£34, 1 shilling*

*and it is signed T
         the mark of Thomas Gilbert*

to Katherine Harrison

Deare Kate

We've rented an untamed place by the Great Meadow. Our larder's empty, our harvest seized. Thomas took us to visit the cellar house to find his hidden ale. Pushed open the door, saw it's taken over by a red fox and her pups — their den the earthen space which held our beds. Her eyes glowed in the fading light. I named her Henrietta, for her gazed looked as protective for her babes as Henry's was for me.

Lydea Gilbert
2 November 1651

Pitch Pine Forest, Windsor 1652

Bluebird

Lydea

I see an azure bird while hunting candlewick leaves,
preening himself and his peach breast in a bower, thickly leaved.

I find a copper woman dressed in golden hide,
and think she kneels in prayer betwixt the leaves.

I watch her whisper, twisting scraps and strings
around the furry plants, while collecting twigs and leaves.

She bestows her gifts and marks theirs, gratefully.
Sensing my presence, she looks my way, turns and leaves.

Now Lydea, you must walk with softer steps and open eyes,
carry threads to mark what you pick and what you leave.

Grinding

Lydea

In Indian Neck I discover a pond — blue
and clear, a group of circled rocks beside its hill.

While sitting still, the copper woman joins me, lifting
two smooth, shaped stones from the ground.

Opening her bag, she pours dried corne.
On a hollowed stone she begins to pound fine meal.

I imitate her steady pull of stone
to stone with dry grain between.

Our ears open to the wind's voice
in the dry grass and leaves. Wordlessly, we speak.

The sun traverses the sky; as the light
begins to wane, she pours a part into a bag, gives it to me.

On the pond two leaves, one rust, one golden,
are split apart by currents to travel separately.

The Birth of Rebekah Harrison
1654

Mother Apple
Kate

Bursting with child, my belly
stretched like the skin of a ripe apple.

Today we harvest our fall crop.
John makes me sit cross-legged in the orchard,

my skirts spread like a table across folded knees,
the great collecting sails scattered under the trees

John climbs, making the tree quake.
A rain of *Maiden's Blush* falls to the tarps below.

Baskets, buckets and barrels fill
with autumn's bounty. John brings

me one, with its wash from red to green,
It squirts beneath my teeth.

Juice coats my chin. He covers me with kisses,
calling me the mother apple of his family tree.

The First Birth

I.

Kate

My labor begins in the creamery,
where I contemplate the hard bulges
of my nipples while tugging cow udders.

Pain grabs me. Walking back, I near stumble.
John sends for Aunt Lydea. Till she comes
I imagine her voice, *The first birth goes slowly.*

Let's just keep moving. I perform my morning
tasks, stopping every few minutes to practice
the breath I watched Lydea teach so many women.

John shows concern. I offer reassurance.
Lydea arrives past midday. I've held
the meal and stand to serve bread and cheese.

So calm, I do not know myself,
telling her my pains are still distant.
I watch as she prepares the bed, and checks my belly.

Well done dear girl, well done.

II.

Lydea

This time the midwife confesses
to her daughter in travail.

Between her pains, I whisper
the story of my native friend.
I call her Starmaker for the scarified
pox marks on her forehead turned
astral with knife rays.

I tell her about our wanderings —
the great singing hawk,
the mushroom caps I've eaten
with her guidance, and the great forest cat
we watched stalking and devouring a stag.

When each pain comes, Kate
becomes alert, unafraid,
breathing skillfully as a jester
dancing on his hands.

Tell me how she looks—
I talk of burnt-sugar skin, jet black hair,
soft doeskin and cobalt beads as blue as sky.
I stroke my girl's face and she begins to pant again.

III.

Kate

She helps me rest
and ride the pains
as they close
tighter
telling me stories
my mind can
return to
with each
cramping swell.

My eyes focus on
our carved oak chest
the streak of late day
sun across the wall
the pumpkin
in the corner

The pain's so

visceral,
as if a pick,
deep inside
my being
is pulling
me apart,
while my breath
helps me deny it.

Soon Lydea tells
me to push,
the baby's coming—
and with a final
gathering of effort,
I feel the slip,
the sliding.

IV.

Lydea

Guiding her, Katherine pushes to this world
a grandchild and daughter birthed
through mine and Starmaker's hands.

Windsor 1654

Years pass. My hair streaked
with ash clouds. I've tilled, spun, healed.
How have I been seen?

Lydea

Injury

Lydea

Passing Hayden Corners with no one to answer
the ferry bell, I led the ox as he pulled
the line. I stumbled in the mud and the ox
stepped on me. They thought my back was broken.

Lying ill, I woke one night
to Starmaker's hands, like wren wings
brushing air. From a gourd vial, she filled
a shell dish, lifting it to my mouth. Tasting
new green, it warmed me, and the aching
in my body eased. She held up four fingers.
I shook my head, not grasping her meaning.

Did she mean four shells a day? I nodded,
my eyelids falling, as sleep wrapped
its arms around and drew me deep.

The Widow Bliss

Lydea

Came from Springfield, to stay near
us awhile. Beneath her coif, swirling yellow
curls, appear as a golden halo in the sun.

Often at our door, she asks to help
me with milking, spinning, tending
the fire, spinning or baking.

She is always here at midday meals, bringing
bowls of well-seasoned food to the table,
where Thomas studies her.

She redirects the flow of sorrow from our losses,
and gives the day a feel of early summer,
fresh, and full of prospects.

This evening, Thomas let me know
he'll guide her back to her home, up
the Great River, along the edge of the white waters.

My Pockets
Lydea

My pockets carry sentimental pieces.
These womb-shaped bags hang below my skirts
hiding needed things, tools for nourishing,
locks of my children's hair and linen strings.

These womb-shaped bags hang below my skirts
protecting simple, precious things —
locks of my children's hair and linen strings,
a sharp blade, scrap cloth squares.

Protecting simple, precious things,
wrapped in a piece from my mother's shift—
a sharp blade, scrap cloth squares,
scattered bones I gathered on the Green.

Wrapped in a piece from my mother's shift,
remnants of loss and change, I spread before me —
scattering bones I gathered on the Green,
arranging the lasting bits from things extinct.

Remnants of loss and change, I spread before me —
hiding needed things, tools for nourishing —
arranging the lasting bits from things extinct.
My pockets carry sentimental pieces.

Mud Flat Wells

Lydea

My Cornish mother was a seamstress,
her needle made costumes for the Globe.
As a babe, I rode her back, or dangled
from a backstage pillar, while she mended
gowns and doublets ripped by stage swords.

Solstices she'd take me home. Full moons
we walked with Grandmam to the shore.
At the lowest tide we'd find the holes
lined with white stones—coastal wishing
wells, shining with light.

We tossed dream talismans inside—
me, a scrap of Holland cloth in wishes for a frock;
mother, a bit of rope to bring my father back;
Grandmam, my braided locks, in promise to forsee.

Secreted Things
Lydea

There are things we don't remember, secreted profoundly
in our hearts, where days of labors, days of caring,
distant journeys and harvest seasons let them hide
below our memory. But today, in the lower meadow,

I stood beside the river, gathering white
crane feathers below their nesting tree,
and recalled my Grandmam, King James' soldiers,
and his witch-hunt that extended as far as Cornwall beach.

Dancing on the sand in the whitest moonlight—
I, a girl in blossom, long hair loose, and
the dance, a rite, from our ancestors,
entreating good harvests at the spring equinox—

the strand bleached by moonglow.
the way our long hair lifted as we turned.
Suddenly, a fearsome yell—*Run. Run
to the cavern!* Horse hooves pounded the sand.

I ran fast. Looking back, I saw the soldiers
tying Grandmam's wrists and ankles, dragging
her across the sand and up the cliff,
making a witch's pyre at the precipice.

September 1654
Lydea

The pond — a black mirror, sprinkled
in leaves, scarlet and gold. Starmaker
and I work in silence. Dry leaves
sing, we are satisfied to listen.

Monarchs rest in goldenrod beside the water.
Heavier of heart than ever I eat
dried deer and berries from her pouch,
and find a bit of peace.

Late, I journey back with a doeskin
pocket she helped me stitch. Crossing
rocky hill, I see a pied cow, the sinking
light coloring its spots with rose and azure.

Never guessed I'd find the Constable and a crowd
of Goodwives waiting. *There she is, the Witch.*
Pointing. *Witch, witch, witch*, their voices chime.
Francis Stiles' wife is with them.

Lydea Gilbert, y'are guilty of suspicion of witchcraft.
Constable knocks my herb basket aside,
binds my wrists and makes me climb
into a cart bound for Hartford jail.

Who'll milk the cow and tend the corne?

— Not the Gilbert witch who brought death to Henry Stiles.

Along rough roads, my mind reviews
their scathing faces — the mothers I midwifed,
the children I delivered, sneering families
I nursed through pox, fevers and flux.
Wind shakes the last leaves off the oaks,
eating through my woolens. Beneath
my petticoat, the softness of white doeskin.

Hartford 1654

Filled with Fury
Kate

Why don't you stand and fight?
      I've come to Hartford
            filled with fury.

How can you kill a man,
      when you're nowhere by?
      And to call it witchcraft three years later?

Why are you just sitting
            silent, without protest?

How does she bear this bleak cell
      a window too high
      to see more than a sky patch,
            her filth straw pallet?

From my skirts I pull two limes,
      Suck sparingly,
            keep away the scurvy.

Her mute thanks.
      An embrace. *Do not worry for me,*
            give kisses to Rebekah.

I never return.
      Her honor's death
            torments me.

24 November 1654
Lydea

The Magistrates wear lace collars to read their verdict.
The Magistrates wear clean, white linen lace.
They sit. I stand on legs weak and trembling.
I've lived in darkness weeks, months. It seems eternal.

The Magistrates wear clean, white linen lace.
Lydea Gilburt thou art here indicted not having the fear of
God, for thou hast given entertainment to the great enemy
of God. His helpe hast killed Henry Stiles' body.

I see my torn and dirty hems, hose and cuffs.
The Magistrates wear clean, white linen lace.
Besides other witchcrafts according to God's law
thou deservest death. In clean, white linen lace,

they ask for words from me. What's there to say?
I gaze as demons dressed in pure pressed linen lace
condemn me, decide I can no longer live,
while Satan smirks across each liar's face.

The Only Salve
Lydea

It is over now. The verdict has been read,
my hanging set for December—

the time I used to try and make small gifts
for my family, and soak a pudding in strong drink.

I feel stabbed through and through,
with no salves for my festering wounds.

I am in darkness. I have not seen a sky or pond.
I've been named God's enemy.

The darkness fills this box of cell, and beside
the rats in putrid straw, I have no friends.

I find my mind is leaving here
and traveling to where my babies wait,

to where Richard reaches out,
and Henry winks and tips his hat to me.

The only salve to cure these bitter sorrows
is the juice of wild memory.

I rub its oils in my palms,
steam it slow as humors rise,

packing each wound
with elaborate memories.

Shadowed

Lydea

Tonight a big white moon shines in the dark.
I imagine the form of Alyse Young shadowed on the wall.

Shadow, I have trembled here
and never felt your shade.

But you were here, weren't you, Alyse,
with your red oak hair and silly tunes?

They took you to this dungeon hole where no music plays,
unless a drip on damp stone and rat scratching make for song.

Alyse, I never warned you.
Maybe then I thought I could believe their words.

Believe in promises—I did, didn't you?
I should have warned you—only sing inside your head.

Don't put breath to it. They took your breath
away, and mine is almost waste.

All beyond late. Alyse does your figure
shade the path of our escape?

Counting
Lydea

At the end of this life
all I can think is tomorrow
will give me a taste of light and sky.

This long imprisonment
I've counted the things
I watched leaving—
one husband, always gone,
three apple-cheeked
cream skinned
babies, who latched
on and laughed, then
died in fever, hot
bodies seizing.

I count the meadows,
the rivers,
the years tending
the cows, the churn,
the yellow cream, and
Henry.

I count the babes I put
to breast, the labors sweat,
the smiles of delight's relief,
knowing I had a hand in
bringing life to fruit.

I count my love for Kate
whose disgrace for me
is writ upon her face.
I will not let love falter here,
for all of us meet
the shame and pain of leaving.

My regret's to hang in winter—I wish
to see a spring rose bloom against the sky.

Lydea's Submission

I bow to your authority — I will be pliant

I bend to your yoke — I will carry

I labor for your nourishment — don't ignore me

I subdue the darkness — treat me lightly

I lean in to listen — don't deny me

I delivered your son, saved your wife — thank me

I answer when you call — don't curse me

Obedient, in your house of prayer — My God is love

I entreat Him to protect my world — while you doubt me

Submitting to your gallows — you won't end me

December 1654
Kate

All I see — Lydea, standing
brave as she is brought before the
gallows.   Witness, I am —

Scared to watch, but Jonathan and
John insisted, *She's been your one
mother, you must look on for her.*

Cold December. Walking, hands tied —
scanning faces, weary eyes. Hers
settled onto mine. The roaring

yells from people, hot for bloodshed
ceased. Her radiance — that warmth
she always gave to women's labor,

glowed as when she nursed the dying.
Look, her eyes, they speak — *Don't grieve me
passing, going on, embracing absent family.*

They place the noose and kick the stool below.
All I see — flaxen-headed babes, who reach out,
to hold her hands from worlds beyond.

Wethersfield 1654-1666

On My Own
Kate

I.

Aunt Lydea is truly gone.
I thought that I could live
without her presence, but being with child
again, I wish I could feel her hands.

The story of the Native woman
who became her friend sticks with me.
I want to find this woman Lydea knew
in the years before her end.

Jonathan works as a translator
among the tribes. I tell him her story,
ask if he'll inquire up river, and
teach me the river peoples' language.

Quite busy with trade and travel, he
brings me Reverend Williams'
treatise on native language. I begin.

II.

Do mermaids understand the choir of whale song?
Or comb their hair with sea-foam, while
marveling at the thickness of the English mind?

Some evenings Jonathan comes for my lessons.
After I scrape plates to the dogs, and
tuck Rebekah in, John sits beside me
with a pipe of Wethersfield tobacco,
and holds my hand as I try to learn a new tongue.

I work to learn the simple words-
Oka'su for mother, *ano'ckqus* for star
peey'aush ne'top, to say, come hither, friend.

Mary Gilbert
Kate

Despite my sweet marriage,
I taste the bile of jealousy
when Jonathan gets a wife.

Daughter of a trader across the sound.
John is open in his joy.
Let's make a picnic.

The devil-hearted part of me
imagines this Mary as ugly
or overbearing.

I swallow hard, forcing
envy down with a cup
of cold creek water.

Before seeing her, I hear her sing,
Over the hills and a long way off
the wind shall blow my top-knot off.

An elfish size, her coif allows
wild black curls to poke out
from slightly stained linen.

Hands, muddied and full
of strawberries. How rare
to hear such laughter.

She runs to me, throws her arms
about me—*Sweet cousin—*
little kisses on my cheeks.

Then apologies—*Excuse my*
excitement— I was hoping
for a friend in this lonesome

colony. Jonathan says you will

love me. All my bile turns
to honey. We ride to the black

rock at Glastonbury. Mary spreads
her scavenged delicacies. Berries
and mushrooms, with sweet cream, and

a cider made from golden
russets. No one to watch us, so
Mary leads our voices in old songs.

Her lilting voice frees me. Riding home
the river becomes a coral snake. In the falling
light, I'm lifted from all envy.

A Liquid Journey
Kate

Mary's my midwife as I bring little Sarah to
life in this world. I remember Rebekah's soft

birthing and try again — riding the pulls in my
belly. They feel like the wildest of waves, awash

over the Truelove's deck rail on our ocean's sail.
Lonesome, Lydea not here with me. Reaching out

over the gray place to lands where the dead reside,
thinking I feel her hands reach out from rough seas to

quiet my shuddering limbs. I'm no stranger to the
mysteries labor can bring. In the minutes that come between,

first, I keep moving and making things orderly,
smooth and neat around me. Then, to our bed I go,

follow these watery dreams — I am plunging low.
glimpsing the treasures there, swimming beside this child,

gliding through a passageway, leading to grottos where
light shines on chests, full of sunken gems, gold bounties.

Mindful my journey contains all the power of
opening pains, and the knowledge of clamping pulls.

Mary calls,
> *It's Pushing time.   Bear on down.   Lift your arms.*
> *Embrace this red-faced,   sweetly wiggling girl.*

Verdant

Kate

With two daughters now, one toddling,
one in arms, and both at my breasts,

I dreamed myself dressed as a native
woman, in hide skirt with naked chest.

I dreamed each girl was nursing a fountain
of milk flowing onto the earth from my nipples.

These became a rivulet, and then a creek,
and finally they flowed into a wide river.

I stood in a verdant pasture, where many creatures
watched us—fat rabbits, flying geese, dun mares,

even white spotted leopards basked in observation,
while my little ones lifted their voices to sing.

Sweet Bodied Years
Kate

I.

Three daughters. I find
I've become like Lydea —
the local doctor.

Bid for births, breast pain,
fever, ague, pox and dropsy,
I call up her ways.

Motherhood wakes my
care, like everyone is mine.
Ah, sweet-bodied years!

II.

Bees fill the hives, golden
syrup drips summer heat. Richness.
Sticky face retreat.

Near harvest, our corne's
red tops thrill my girl's fancies —
sweet flat-cake mornings.

III.

Bobcat eyes the girls
see in the wood — golden leaves,
only ripened pears.

Most wives pray for sons,
girls are my delights — dewy
web dances, story nights.

My tousled creatures,
cuddle to tell us their dreams
waking from sleep's flights.

IV.

A hard rain tonight,
wild winds twisting inky trees—
sounds of whimpering.

I climb from John's side
to the girls' sleeping garret.
I can remember

how branches bending,
and a rainy rooftop din
gives young ones great fright.

Sensing me, they roll
aside, I squeeze between. They
throw arms over me,

fall back to sleep. Rage
Storm! I am alone, awake—
a mast amidst babes.

Abdominal Distemper
Kate

I.

What fools we were to think ourselves
insulated from tragedy. John returned
from the Sound, doubled over in belly pain.

I tended him with crushed poppy seed
and soon he seemed to heal, drank my broths
without ache, nausea or flux. Later, he rose from our bed.

We even made gentle love one day, alone,
mid-afternoon, as a goose roasted on the spit—
long-lovers by the fire.

Then, he made me call for Jonathan and Josiah,
kissed my forehead and shooed me
so the men could speak.

II.

A storm builds
across the river.
Black clouds
and I am closed out.

Deep worry. Hours
ago, the men began meeting.
I sit on the stairs

watching a row of ants
carry crumbs of dry biscuit—
such perfect order.

Inside my chest
gray layers race

like this wild sky.
Whispers and shouts.
Why do they leave me out?

The winds shake leaves,
make them mumble,
make then scream.

For an instant, a swirling cloud
bloom opens wide and sun shoots
a vision through blue-white.

These days I worried how
I'd live without him, no
better with dark swirls and
twisting, cracking branches.

Elegy

6 September 1666
Kate

Gone—
my lover, partner, helpmate, husband,
wise man, beloved papa, dear friend—
gone. We had three happy weeks—
August apple harvests.
Next, he clenched his belly and turned
from ruddy-gold to cold-wash-water
gray, his skin clammy, breath labored.
I tried, but my herbs, my poultices,
even my body wrapped naked around
his to calm the quaking chills, did nothing.
He died, me holding him.

Oh, grieving fields,
inconsolable daughters,
braying calves, and I, alone—
never to feel his warmth,
never to banter-barter in lively debate—
planning for the farm, the girls, the orchards.

He always listened to my thoughts, considered
my opinions, let me choose. Like equals.
Never again such raptured liberty—
he swings me high, showers kisses, dances me.
Gone, one who lavished joy, shared fantastic tales,
made us an island of family.

No consolation,
no condolence but to complete
the harvest and keep at daily caring.

The Reading

John Harrison's Will

Cast of Characters:
Katherine (Kate) Harrison
Jonathan Gilbert, first cousin and friend
Josiah Gilbert, first cousin
Setting:
A large oak table before a fireplace.
Kate, distraught, sits between her cousins.
Jonathan reads from a sheet of parchment

Jonathan

I John Harrison doe make my last Will & Testament.
I give to my eldest daughter Rebekah £60,
to Mary my 2ⁿᵈ daughter £60, to Sarah £60
My estate I leave to my wife and make her sole Executrix.

Kate
This is not done.
Josiah
I told John so,
that I did not agree.

Jonathan
He wanted this.
You were the only one he trusted
to complete his dreams.

Kate
I want John back, not his things.

Jonathan
But they were always yours,
you were a partnership, a union. Resolve
to remain the woman he believed in.

Wethersfield 1666-1668

First Blood

Kate

Oh, daughter, oh, woman,
oh, child of mine,
your flowers
are blooming,
let's have a red time.

Circle white sand round
your childhood bed,
walk the path of petals
and peelings,
all red.

Burn beetroot candles,
with sumac and madder
dye your skirts
fruiting red.

Soft cattail cushions
will soak your flux.
Bury them deep
amid carrots
and turnips.

Oh, Daughter
your flowers
are blooming
in reds.

Bee Whisperer
Kate

For weeks we've seen some wild winds.
Today, I find my hives knocked over.
A season's honey smeared in rivers
on the ground. I stand their domes again.

The bees are swarming in the trees and fighting
against the gale. I watch one entire colony
trapped by a whirlwind, carried out and up
across the Green. I run to follow and see them
swept over the river and caught in a maple grove.

Can anyone call bees?

Alone before the water's edge,
in desperate worry for my colony,
not knowing what to do, I hold
my arms high, as if to block the wind,
and cry like swarming bees. I speak
about our apple blooms, promise
them acres of blossoms and honey mounds.

Your domes are upright, your babies waiting.

Suddenly, in one black cloud, they return
across the water, above my raised
head and waving arms, over the Green.

When I return, almost
horizontal against the raging winds,
I climb to my orchard, and find
the hives filling
with colonies of bees.

Damnified

Kate

I feel smashed, like my pumpkins were. Crushed
in the garden by Griswold and his horses. Beheld
them destroying my fields—the fat pumpkins, a vale
full of ripe and expecting wombs, glowed in the sun.
Now, they're damnified.　　　　Ruined.

Yes, I cursed that foul Griswold. All heard me. I cursed
his cold wife as well, screaming accusations at me, while I
could still see his men laughing and trampling my crop.
Like the Crowned Head's own soldiers, they kill as they split
through pregnant bellies of seed. So filled
with their power.　　　　Destroyed.

So, I tell him he'll go to the devil—his wife, as well. There's
no protection for us around here any longer.
It's cracking my heart.　　　　So, I yell.

Thirsted After

Kate

A woman alone, with three maiden
daughters—the marriage stock men thirst for.

Rebekah is fifteen and my other girls are close to seeing
their first blood, and my heart can't break from John.

After I refuse suitor after suitor for myself
and my daughters, we are turned against.

This morning in the barn, I found my ox
bored through with something like a crude drill,

its entrails strewn across the floor, its moans
so human, that I must slit its throat

to stop the pain. A rape of sorts, warning me
not to remain a widow, unwed, with land and money.

Blinded by Tears
Kate

A few days later, I hear men in the night
coming near my door.
I think I recognize the voice
of neighbor Bracy.

Drunken, they discover Ophelia,
my cream giving cow, with her calf
asleep beside her, and slit her bag
with a pitch fork.

She screams as she stumbles.
Her calf whimpers.
My girls and I hide, trembling,
until the men are gone.

My daughters stroke Ophelia,
whispering sweetly, as I kneel
in her blood, trying to staunch and
stitch her wound.

I ask Rebekah
to remove the calf,
for its moan is so painful.
I'm blinded by tears.

We will have to feed
it gruel now,
for this one will
never nurse again.

Oh John, why did you
leave me with no son?
For our beautiful land
I am cursed.

The Chase
Kate

a hawk flies through pursued
                  by a small bird
coming so close to me I see

                               its eye and dappled
                                        tawny-white
                               beneath its wing

this self-same raptor
                  circles overhead
and sings to me

                               stately bird of prey
                                        why race
                               from a bird so small

   you could
                  break it with
your talons.

                               oh, hawk don't
                                        leave please
                             cry again to me

Body of Thorns
Kate

In Fearful Swamp, I searched for my calf,
stolen from its safe place, under the apple,

beside the barn, near our door.
I thought I heard commotion in the night.

and this morning, saw the prints
of two men's feet heading south. I left

my girls abed, followed large boot
prints and hoof marks' draw and drag

into a briar forest. Thick and deep,
in needled barbs, I found him—bound

in green vines, trussed in bladed
thorns, twisted in, struggling to escape.

His torn hide dripped blood. Now, I,
alone, must free him from this mangled fate.

So like my girls, I begin to sing a nursery song,
Ring around the rosies, as I gently lift and pull

each thorn, and try to toss the vines aside.
They catch my coif, snag my waistcoat

and rip my cheek. I stroke my calf and keep singing
my song, *Ashes, ashes, we all fall down.*

A Different Way
Kate

Not knowing what to do any longer—
filled up with loneliness and fear,
I feel there is no where to turn;

so I start to gather pale stones.
When I fill a manageable sack, and the moon
is almost waxed full, I walk at night

to the soft earth near the river. Remembering
Lydea's stories, I dig on my knees, making
a hole an arm's length deep, and begin

to line the edges with my stones. Midnight,
the moon overhead, and my finished hole gleams.
Now I put symbols for my wishes inside.

I have brought a clip of cloth from John's coat,
and a lock of each girl's hair. With my knife,
I slice a good piece of my own, braiding them together,

tying off with the yarn from John's coat scrap.
I plead for our little family's protection,
for John to wrap us in his arms.

Then, I work my plait into a ball of clay,
drop it in the glowing well I made. Despair can drive
us to the night, to seek a different way to pray.

5 May 1668

Kate

How much worse can it become?
Life is Hades without John, then

I am dragged from my bed, one morning,
bound and accused of witchcraft.

Oh, Lydea, I see now. My troubles
multiply like pomegranate seeds,

red as blood, they cling to me.
I hear the guards saying they waited

for Jonathan to sail past the Sound
before arresting me. Guards mumble, *Satan.*

I see his works quite clear, my captivity
and confinement—acts he's commandeered.

Hartford 1668

Unanswerable Questions
Kate

Days pass
below the earth.
A barred window.

Darkness.

Black nights, dank hay,
rats that eat better than I,
who bleakly wait.

What brought me to this place?

If I could have learned to
hold my tongue, would I be
somewhere else—not imprisoned,

awaiting certain death?

Or, are these questions
worthless as the rank dust
below my fingers?

What are the truths?

I used my voice.
I said *No*, no thanks—
I can maintain my own house,

my own land.
I will not marry you,
I will not give you Rebekah,

or allow our girls of nine
and twelve years
into some old man's bed—

Then one by one

the damage comes—
cut, shattered, stabbed, destroyed.

I could not be silent.
I cursed back. What have I done?

Accused, jailed as I am,
I still would have spoken—
refused a loveless marriage,

refused to make
my daughters
property.

4 October 1669
Kate

I.

Jonathan
gives me strength.

He comes to my cell
with ink, quill and parchment.

He asks me to address the
Fathers of the Commonweale,

I've been imprisoned half a year.
He wants me to evoke my torments,

from John's passing; to list each injury,
name witnesses, and spare no description of our sufferings.

II.

A Complaint of Several Grievances of the Widow Harrison
 6 October 1669

May this honored court have patience
with me having none to complain to
but the Fathers of the Commonweale.

Meeting with many injuries necessitates
me to look for relief. I am bold to present
you with these lines, I suffer humbly craving your consideration,
(for) the state of my wrongs, (which I conceive are great)

> *A yoke of oxen spoiled at our stile,*
> *blows upon the back and side,*

> *a cow, back broke and two ribs,*

a(nother) cow, at the side yard,
her jawbone broke and a hole bored in her side,

A three-year-old heifer in the meadow, struck
with a knife, wounded to death,

A cow wounded in the bag (as she stood before my
door),

A sow, her hind legs cut off,

My corne, in mile meadow, damnified with horses,

My two-year-old steer, the back broke,

Thirty poles of hops, cut and spoyled,

All injuries do savor of envy (and) happened since my husband's
death.

Witness the oxen Jonathan and Josiah Gilbert;
Witness the cows Josiah Gilbert, Enoch Black,
Witness the heifer Widow Stoddard's son,
Witness the corne John Beckly
Witness the hops Goodwife Standish and Mary Wright.

I hope this honored court judge according to their demerit
and that your bold suppliant will find redress.
   Your servant and suppliant,
    Katherine Harrison

To Court

Kate

My eyes fight
to adjust from dark

Day's brilliance
Beauty burned
in tight squint
Glimpse the fields
harvested and golden

Then dimness
Great room
Dark tables

My vision fights
for clarity
My eyes cannot see

Jonathan's present
in the crowd
His eye catches mine

He has my letter,
but his look
shows no hope.

Thomas Bracy's Testimony

…he saw a cart cominge towards John Harrison's house, and on top of the hay he saw a perfectly red calfe's head… 13 August 1669

Kate

Reveals his guilt—
the story of a vision,
where a red calf's
head turns into myself
riding in a hay wagon.

So, he cannot forget
what he did to us,
how the blood
from Ophelia's bag
covered her calf,
how he watched me
from a distance,
kneeling
in the dirt and straw.

Now, when his visions
stop his hands from
piecing a coat correctly
he's remembering
our sow and chopping
off her legs.

Elizabeth Cullick Smith's Testimony

...the wife of Simon Smith testified that Katherine
told her fortune, that her husband's name should be
*Simon...*28 September 1669

Kate

My former bedmate, Bess Cullick
testifies against me, saying I am a notorious
liar, Sabbath breaker, and teller of fortunes.

Near twenty year ago, she asked me
in the bedclothes one cold night,
Who will my husband be? Simon says,
begging, *Now tell me!*

Well, if Simon says, I teased,
then that's who it'll be.

She testifies no linen yarn was ever finer
or faster spun. True enough. She always
pleaded for me to finish hers,
Please Kate, my mother's so particular.
Being dear God-Sib to her, I always would agree.

Twisted Silence
Kate

I named Josiah,
who used to play with me
in the hay hills on the Malvern farm,
requesting he testify for me.

I called him to bear witness.
His refusal to visit the court,
his black twisting silence,
feels like a poisoned dart.

Is this the same cousin
who at age five, kissed me
and said that he would always be
my knight and I, his Lady?

He sent, in his place,
a man who testified
Goodman Gilbert
says he knows not of me,

that I am no cousin to him,
and added that he heard I
followed the armies back in England.
Called me whore.

I grow weak and shudder.
Dear cousin, who helped drag the carcass of my steer,
What killed your courage?
What do you fear?

Rebecca Smith's Testimony

Rebecca Smith aged about 75 years testifieth Good wife Gilbert the Wife of Jonathan Gilbert had a cap she refused to sell to Katherine, after Goodwife Gilbert wore said cap her head and shoulders were much afflicted...Rebecca Smith heard say the cap was burned. 12 October 1668

Kate

Making apple
butter Mary
and I'd became
easily silly
peeling cutting
orb after orb
red yellow
spotted green
smooth streaked

Taking a week
vats simmered
smelling sweet
and spice

Waving flies
away we sang
rounds of reckless
giggling

Our running
joke—the hat
we tossed back
and forth—
calling it
      top-knot
swap-knot
      glop knot
stock pot
      blot knot
forgot-it-not—

Mary's black curls
amassed in tangles
vat steamed
made wild by
tossing the cap

Thick apple butter
plopped on
the fires
crocks washed
and ready
for pouring
shelves filling
in cellars enough
to share with all

Forgot there's some
who take offense
and find Satan's
touch in unbridled
friendships.

Sentenced

Kate

I stand before them.
They read their verdict.
Strong men all, and half whom
I suspect did violence against me.

What makes me so important,
as if in this world of rivers,
trees and earth there is not enough
for all to share?

I watch the Magistrates, Governor Winthrop and the rest,
arrange themselves to hear the verdict
and decide my sentence. All sit, while I, weakened
by six months in darkness, must stand.

We find Kateran Harrison
guilty of witchcraft,
and familiarity with Sathan,
the grand enemie of God and mankind.

Hanging is the punishment, yet the Magistrates
confer and confer, then choose to wait
to carry out my sentence until they bring
some questions from my case before the Ministers.

These strong men, all well fed and cushion seated,
choose to reconvene this coming spring.
Facing six more months imprisoned
I stumble to my knees.

Hartford 1669

My Nightmare
Kate

I try to contact Starmaker,
the female sachem of the tribe,
Lydea's friend. I seek her through a twisted
path, shrouded by tangled vines.

She heard of my desire to meet her,
and now she is coming. I try to warn
her, but my frozen body cannot call out.
I see her wandering the Fearful Swamp.

The men who despise us wait
with their muskets and swords. Grey
muck stains her white moccasins.
I try again to call, *Go back. Go back.*

She does not hear, she keeps on—straight
and strong along the vicious path.
When I wake, she is nowhere, but fears remain,
imprinted on this rot straw where I sleep.

Smelling Spring
Kate

This morning I woke from fitful sleep
and smelled, fresh and new upon the air,
the scent of plowing. It drifted on
a breeze through my little light shaft,
accompanied by an aviary celebration—
robins singing, spreading sweet worm words.

Feeling I've been broken, plowed like dormant soil,
I draw my breath deep, finding whiffs—
narcissus, lilac, hyacinth and apple.

I lean against a bit of wall, opposite
the window slit where the breezes bring delight.
I close my eyes, and I am almost with them,
the Gilberts with oxen and plow, and my
daughters, following with song and seed.

Citizens of Wethersfield
Kate

May horns grow from your angelic gravestones;

May rose thorns pierce your soft-soled slippers;

May bees swarm your breeches;

May your fresh milk spoil and clot;

May your ripe pumpkins burst open with goblin babies;

Mangled in the Fearful Swamp, may your carcass be
lost until it's turned to bone;

May assaulted housemaids fill your throats with coals;

May your daughters rebel and run away for love;

May the spring floods wash your seeds to sprout
downriver on native ground;

May your animals turn against you, bite
and shake you;

May your head be filled with lewd songs
bursting from your lips and never cease;

May your couplings be filled with love and
set your hearts aflame, so your losses make you shatter;

May the damages you've done return a hundred-fold
for every maiden you frightened with blood and pain;

And may I return from the hereafter, whispering
your cruelties to any visitor who'll say—*My, what a lovely town.*

for John
Kate

I can tell you there were years
when happiness rained on us—
such blissful deniers —sorrow always comes;

I can say we were blessed with three
living daughters; I can say we knew
love—deep, abiding, until death took you;

I can tell you your passing and your faith
in me has left me caustic and unyielding
to some, yet generous, whimsical, hopeful,
and defending as a lioness for our girls;

I can tell you didn't know you'd make
these people hate me and try their best
to ruin me, while I stood firm and brave
as you thought me;

I must tell you I am ruined, thoroughly,
but our girls are free, not forced
into some joyless coupling.

I believe this is my legacy—
to end in ruin, to be sent before the gallows
come morning, but to know my loud,
lawless resistance set our girls free;

I can tell you I believe our love lives,
does not surrender. Because I did not
yield, it lives on;

I can say this is my leaving, my last
word, spoken to this cold cell, never
forgetting our dances, our laughter,
the love we made.

The Court of Assistants 20 May
Kate

Today I return to Court.
Last night I heard
my sentence will finally come.

I slept the fitful sleep of those who wait
the final danger, dreaming seabirds, their necks
entangled, tumbling from the clouds into a raging sea.

My life is almost ended,
but before the last, I'll get to see the spring.
Despite imprisoned weakness,

I want to stand tall as Mistress Hutchinson.
As they lead me before the Magistrates, I am
mesmerized by sunlight streaming across the room.

Not asked to speak, I imagine my final
moment smelling green grass, new wheat
and apple blossoms once again.

The Governor begins to speak,
his words filter slowly
through my speech starved mind:

*We have considered the verdict of the jury and cannot concur to
sentence her to death, but pay just fees, and remove from Wethers
Field to tend her safety and the contentment of her neighbors.*

I still await my hanging date, when I find my wrists
are loosed of hemp, the space about me emptied,
and an attendant whispering to me, *Get on now, thou art free.*

Walking
Kate

Freed from my year alone I feel my voice.
        My bones ache, but I know my fears can die.

Though each step aches, I know I will not die.
        I had a wild spirit wanting to ride winds.

Today my wild spirit rides bright winds
        finding despair's opposite in a single hawk.

My despair lifts with that screeching hawk,
        shame banished as apples bloom and calves call.

The trees will fruit, the cows will nurse their calves.
        From rebirth's pains, I find I'm lifted up.

From labor's ceaseless pains I'm lifted up
        and race until my arms enclose my daughters.

I race till I again embrace my daughters.
        Freed from my year alone I feel my voice.

Author's Notes/ Acknowledgements

Lydea Gilbert and Katherine (Kate) Harrison were real women who lived along the Connecticut River in the mid-1600's. Their stories mainly exist in court records, including probate records and the transcripts of their trials, which outline the barest bones of their lives.

When my life partner, Bill Tankersley, an historian and genealogist, first discovered Lydea's history, he told me, "One of your ancestors was found guilty of witchcraft", I was both drawn to and repelled from telling the story. I remembered my family's visitsto our Gilbert relatives in southern Illinois as a young girl, but I had a great distaste for what I had learned about the Puritan history of early New England.

Bill directed my research with a set of readings, opening my eyes to the complexities of early America. I offer gratitude to the book, *1491,* by Charles Mann, who elucidated a vision of Indigenous New England before European settlement. I learned so much from historical archaeologists James and Patricia Scott Deetz, who documented their discoveries in *The Times of Their Lives: Life, Love and Death in Plymouth Colony.* My visit to their re-created *Plimoth Plantation* and *the Mayflower* opened my senses and my imagination to a life far beyond my ken.

My lasting gratitude goes to Laurel Thatcher Ulrich's books on the lives of Colonial women, *Good Wives: Images and Reality in the Lives of Women in Northern New England* and *A Midwife's Tale.* Ulrich taught me how to uncover the undocumented lives of women, through probate and other court records, and material objects such as needlework and pockets. *A Midwife's Tale* was my guide for the experience of women healers. Most of all, I thank her for this book's title, borrowed from a passage in *Good Wives.*

I uncovered many historical events occurring in Windsor, including the corporal punishment of women, and the conflicts between

Henry and Francis Stiles through *The Public Records of the Colony of Connecticut* (1850).

The white stone wells along the shore are real, discovered in the article, *Witches of Cornwall,* by Kate Ravilious in *Archeology Magazine*.

I spent a week's residency at poet Marilyn Nelson's *Soul Mountain Retreat*. I wrote the first draft of poems by the pond and the creek in early September, while at night Marilyn graciously listened to my day's work, and asked the intriguing question, "What if they *were* witches?"

I wrote the initial draft of this book before earning my MFA from Sierra Nevada University, and decided to return to it after the 2016 election. I thank my faculty mentors for opening my heart to poetic form and guiding me to dig deeper into my personal experiences to find my soft, vulnerable self. Consequently, through their teachings, I was able to uncover my characters' deeper selves.

I thank Katherine Harrison for writing an account of her abuse by the Wethersfield community after her husband's death. Although she never knew it, her written voice impacted the American justice system. I learned of Kate's letter to the Magistrates only because of the extensive primary research of David C. Hall, who included the documents of her trial in his book, *Witch-Hunting in Seventeenth-Century New England.*

I thank my first readers—Kelye Lotz, Stephanie Farrow, Anne Bailey and Linda Vega for their earliest questions, and I offer deep appreciation for the poets who critiqued my later drafts in workshops over the years—Jim Mersmann, Maria Vargas, Ashley Hulsey Coutch, Brent Stauffer, Barry Curtis, Abiola Sholanke, Lucy Jaffe, Margaret Marston, Salaam Green, Susan Diane Mitchell, Jasper Kennedy, Che Hatter and Glenny Brock.

Special thanks to Annie Finch, whose workshop, *Working The Beat More; How to Make Poems Sing in Depth,* gave me the final touch of revision magic. My gratitude to Kwoya Fagin-Maples who encouraged me to exercise the power of letting poems go.

I am deeply grateful for my Birmingham poetry community and my reading opportunities with *The Magic City Poetry Festival, Sister City Connection, 100 Thousand Poets for Change, Bards and Brews* and *Birmingham Stands*, where these words first found an audience.

Thanks to these journals for giving the following poems a platform:

Cleaning Garlic, Sonnet for Henry, If This Be Heresy, and Death's Echo, Hobo Camp Review, 2021

A Different Way and *Walking Duplex*, Simple Machines, 2021

Bee Whisperer, Poetry, 2021

A Lashing, Cahoodleloodling, 2019

Before Ministers and Magistrates, Voices of Resistance Anthology, 2017

Thanks to Windsor Historical Society, Windsor, CT for permission to publish the *1640-1654 Plan of Windsor map.*

Special gratitude to Alina Stefanescu Coryell who suggested I embroider the book's cover design, and to Joe Taylor and *Livingston Press* for believing in this story.

Today we are living in a country that is forgetting its history. Some law-makers are legislating against learning our nation's real history, as others attempt to swing us back to times where feminine power and the value of women's lives was suspect and condemned. It is critical that we remember and understand the labors, sacrifices and contributions of the unsung creators of our society, the women, the Indigenous, the enslaved—who built and maintained daily life, and nurtured all to flourish. With these thoughts in mind, I thank the muses of memory, the detectives of research and the shamans of imagination, who joined together in creating Lydea and Kate's story—a labor which has truly been an art, a craft, a mystery.

Laura Secord is a poet, writer, spoken word artist, storyteller and teaching artist. She earned her MFA in Creative writing from Sierra Nevada University. She has worked as a printer, union organizer, health care activist, teacher, sex-educator and nurse practitioner in community health and HIV care. A Pushcart nominee, her poems appear in *Poetry, Hobo Camp Review, Shift, Simple Machines, Cahoodleloodling, Finishing Line Press, Burning House Press, Voices of Resistance, Snapdragon, Indolent Books, Passager, PoemMemoirStory, The Southern Women's Review, The Birmingham Weekly and Arts* and *Understanding*. She serves the Director of Community Engagement for The Magic City Poetry Festival. She teaches poetry to vulnerable citizens in her community, produces poetry events, and maintains a lifetime commitment to sharing unvoiced stories. She lives in a purple house and walks with a leaping dog.